THE
VAMPIRE
QUEST

Simon Cheshire

**FICTION
EXPRESS**

What do other readers think?

Here are some comments left on the Fiction Express blog about this book:

"I love The Vampire Quest *because it entertained me."*
Joshua P, Shropshire

"WOW…that book was amazing.
I loved every second reading it."
Delilah, Norfolk

*"*The Vampire Quest *is amazing and I wish there was more. Thank you for writing it."*
Lucy C, Norfolk

"Firstly we would like to say that The Vampire Quest *is an amazing book. We would like to congratulate the author of the book for keeping us entertained. We hope to read some more of your stories in the future!"*
Whitehall Primary School Year 5 Class 3, Leicester

"This book was fangtastic! We wish The Vampire Quest *had not ended."*
Hazel Class, Crowmore School, Shrewsbury

*"*The Vampire Quest *is a brilliant, fantastic book. Every single chapter is really good and I loved it."*
Lizzie W, Sheffield

Contents

Chapter 1

A Surprise Discovery

It was a Wednesday evening, just after seven o'clock, when James found out that his best mate, Vince Pierce, was a vampire. Vince had been acting strangely at school for a few days, distracted and jittery. James had asked his friend if something was bothering him, but Vince had simply answered that everything was fine, thank you very much, nice of you to ask.

On that Wednesday, James and his parents had just finished their tea when they began to hear noises coming from their neighbour's house. Vince, his mum and dad, and his little sister Val had lived next door to James for as long as he could remember. Normally, the Pierce family were quiet, polite neighbours. Sure, every Hallowe'en they'd have a party full of weird-looking guests (to which James and his parents were never invited), but apart from that they generally kept themselves to themselves.

However, at just before seven pm, loud bangs, scrapes and other sounds began to thud through the wall of James's bedroom. It sounded as if Vince and his family were throwing all the furniture about!

James crept out into the back garden and peered over the fence that divided his house from Vince's. The bangs and bumps continued, and now James could also hear cries of "There must be some around here somewhere!" and "Why didn't you order more last time?" and "If I find you've got some hidden under your bed, young man, you're in big trouble."

At last, Vince stormed out of his house, looking very cross…and very worried. His skin was odd, too. It was always dead pale, but now it was sort of greyish in colour. His eyes looked even darker than usual, and his teeth didn't appear to fit into his mouth properly any more.

James peeped over the fence. "You OK?"

Vince jumped in surprise. "Oh! James, didn't see you there." He straightened his pullover, as if he was embarrassed that James should see him like this.

"There's definitely something the matter," said James. "Can I help? You all seem to be searching for something?"

Vince blinked nervously at James for a moment, then gave a deep sigh. "Yes, we are. We're completely out of…out of Feed'N'Gulp."

"What's that," said James, "some sort of fizzy drink?"

"Ummm," winced Vince, "sort of." Then he let out another sigh and ran his hands through his jet-black hair. "It's no good. Things are so bad that the secret will soon be out. I might as well tell you the truth."

"The truth about what?" asked James, as a tumbling crash echoed from inside

Vince's house and a voice yelled "Oi! How much junk have you stuffed in this cupboard?"

Vince gave James an awkward look, then whispered. "Look. It's like this… um…well…I'm a vampire…So are my mum and dad…and Val."

Chapter 2

A Recipe for Disaster

James stared at Vince for a moment, then burst out laughing. "Yeah, right," he guffawed. "Vince the Vampire. Good one!"

Vince opened his mouth and showed James his teeth. Two of them had suddenly become pointy...*very* pointy...and long. James jumped back in fright, letting out a strange yelp (which was all he could manage under the circumstances).

"B-But how? What? Why?" he stammered at last. "You're my best mate – just an ordinary kid like me. There's nothing spooky about your family. Well, except those Hallowe'en parties. What's going on?"

"Well, you shouldn't always believe everything you see in the movies," sighed Vince. "Vampires have been around for thousands of years," he explained. "In the beginning…we sometimes attacked humans – I can't deny it. But we realized how terribly wrong that was. Nowadays, we're nice, gentle people. We don't want to drink your blood." His face crumpled with disgust at the thought. "Yeuch, that's a horrid thing to do. So, the ancient vampires came up with Feed'N'Gulp. It's a kind of magical potion. Every vampire has to drink half a litre a day. It keeps our teeth at normal size, and allows us to go out in daylight, and stops us getting… you know…hungry."

"Hungry as in…bloodthirsty?" gulped James.

"Exactly," said Vince. "The last thing we'd ever want to do is upset humans by leaping out of the dark and biting their necks. That would be terrible. And quite rude, too."

"I see," said James, going a bit boggle-eyed. "So without this Feed'N'Gulp, the four of you will start going around in black capes with bloodstained fangs?"

"Well, it looks that way," said Vince. "Except there'd be a lot more than four of us. There are loads of vampires all over the world. For a start, the family at No. 38 are vampires too."

"What?" gasped James.

"Yes," said Vince, "haven't you ever wondered why they've got a turret sticking up out of their house with bats flying round it?"

"I thought it was just a funny-looking attic conversion," said James. "But isn't it just your family that's run out of Feed'N'Gulp?"

"Nope, 'fraid not," said Vince. "Normally, you see, we all order it online. The whole world's supply is brewed in a factory owned by the Gulp-It-Down Corporation. But they've been taken over by someone called Dave Van Helsing. He's the great-great-grandson of some Victorian vampire hunter or other. Anyway, he doesn't believe in vampires, and the factory has shut down. No more Feed'N'Gulp. Not ever."

"AARGH!" cried James in a panic. "That means every vampire in the world will soon be thirsting for human blood!"

"Yes," tutted Vince. "It *is* a bit of a nuisance."

"Nuisance?" cried James. "It's a disaster! A catastrophe! Humans and vampires will be fighting each other for eternity! For goodness' sake, why didn't all you vampires tell us the truth about yourselves before?"

"What, with all those books and movies and TV shows making us out to be horrible monsters?" cried Vince. "No thank you. Humans always assume vampires are evil…unless you look like Robert Pattinson – who *isn't* a real vampire by the way! It's very unfair. We've complained to the BBC, but it didn't do any good."

"If the factory's gone," said James, "can't you just brew your own Feed'N'Gulp at home? Or at least, something similar?"

Vince wrinkled his nose. "It's not that easy, I'm afraid. The recipe's a 'closely-guarded' secret. And it's said to contain some rather unusual ingredients like goblins' toenails and trolls' breath. There aren't many trolls around today, you know. If you're lucky you might find one lurking under a motorway flyover or rummaging through the bins behind a fast food restaurant."

"But there must be some way to find the recipe!" said James.

"Well, the good news is, there is still one copy of the recipe," said Vince.

"Great!" said James. "And the bad news?"

"The recipe is carved into stone in a rather terrible, place."

"Go on," urged James, nervously.

"It's somewhere in the Forest Of Infinite Darkness, where Toothcarver the dragon lives."

"Oh dear," muttered James. "That doesn't sound like…(gulp) a charming holiday destination."

"It's not; it's awful," said Vince. "And, as far as I know, no vampire has ever returned from there alive."

By now, darkness had fallen. A full moon shone in the sky. A strange howling could be heard coming from No. 38.

Meanwhile, Vince's teeth seemed to have become a little pointier. He was licking his lips.

"Vampires can only last a couple of days without Feed'N'Gulp," he said sadly. "I'm starting to get terribly peckish already."

James, wide-eyed with fear, took a step or two back....

Chapter 3

Into the Unknown

"Right," said James, pulling himself together "We'd better find this recipe… and quickly."

"You'd really help me out?" said Vince with a tear in his eye. "Even though I just told you I'm a vampire?"

James nodded and Vince smiled, showing his slightly larger, even more pointy teeth.

"Thank you," he said. "You really are a good friend."

"Now then, this Forest Of Infinite Darkness," queried James. "If it's dark, we can creep around it without the dragon seeing us, right?"

"I suppose so," replied Vince. "Although… there was something about Toothcarver the dragon I can't quite remember…."

"Okay, well you think while I get some supplies," said James, heading back towards his house. "I'll meet you out front in a minute."

Dashing upstairs two steps at a time he grabbed a torch, his penknife and a bag of sweets left over from his school lunchbox. Rushing back through the kitchen he reached out and grabbed a bulb of garlic from the bowl by the sink.

Just in case… he thought to himself.

"Umm…where exactly is this forest?" he queried as soon as he was by his friend's side.

"In another world," said Vince. "Don't worry, we can be there in a flash."

Vince suddenly spun on his heels. A weird mixture of smoke and lightning engulfed them, and seconds later, the two of them were standing on a freezing cold hillside. Below them stretched an endless blanket of trees – the Forest Of Infinite Darkness.

"Hmm, not so much a flash, more a whoosh," said Vince.

"Wow," said James, looking down at the gloomy landscape ahead of them. "That's a very useful skill to have."

"Oh, there's a lot more to us vampires than the movies make out," said Vince. "Unfortunately, we can only travel like that when we're desperate for Feed'N'Gulp. Or blood. It's actually quite tiring or I'd go to school like that every day – it'd save a lot of time."

They crept into the forest. The trees were ancient and gnarled, growing close together. Their branches twisted and entwined overhead, almost cutting out the thin, watery daylight completely. The air was cold and still, and a rancid smell of decay hung in the atmosphere. James switched on his torch, but the pale light only made the darkness seem even denser.

"I can hardly see a thing," whispered James. There was a long silence. "Vince? …VINCE?"

"Shhhh!" said Vince. "I'm here. Listen. Can you hear that sound?"

James concentrated. There was a THUMP THUMP of heavy feet and a soft, low rumbling noise coming from up ahead. It sounded like something being dragged along the ground. Then there was a long, slow hiss, like the noise a snoring snake might make. James turned off the torch immediately.

"I've just remembered what it was about the dragon…" whispered Vince.

"And?" whispered James. The sound was getting closer.

"It might be very dark in here, but Toothcarver doesn't need any light. He hunts by smell."

James suddenly wished he hadn't used his mum's SuperFresh NicePong shampoo in the shower that morning. The strange thumping and dragging sound was getting closer by the second. James wondered if they should make a run for it, but with so many trees around them, so close together, running around in the shadowy gloom of the forest didn't seem like a good idea.

Suddenly, a low, rasping voice drifted around the tree trunks. "By my scaly dragon's feet, I sssssmell fresh meat."

James almost screamed with fright. Vince did scream with fright, then clapped his hands over his mouth.

"Sssssteady Toothy sssssteady. It sssssounds like sssssupper's ready," boomed the voice.

A huge shape moved through the darkness beside them. James turned on his torch and shone it upwards just in time to see a huge set of fangs. Toothcarver smiled menacingly down at them. He loomed over James and

Vince, his gigantic forked tongue licking his lips. His eyes were like shiny black marbles, and his body was as twisted as the trees. A pair of spidery wings flexed and flapped above his back.

"Good evening, my sssssweeties," hissed Toothcarver. "My two little treaties."

Chapter 4

A Dragon's dinner?

"T-T-This is why no v-v-vampire has ever c-come back from h-h-here alive," stuttered Vince. "Raw v-v-vampire's his favourite meal!"

"Leg it!" yelled James. They'd have to make a run for it in the shadowy gloom of the forest after all. Otherwise they'd be eaten!

The beam from the torchlight bouncing ahead of them, James and Vince ran as fast as their shaking legs would carry them. They jumped over roots, dodged around tree trunks and flung branches aside as they fled. Toothcarver slid after them, dragging himself along by his enormous claws.

"Let's just zap out of here!" cried Vince.

"No, the Feed'N'Gulp recipe is in this forest somewhere," gasped James. "If we don't find it here, we'll only have to face greater dangers somewhere else."

"Greater than being gobbled up by a dragon?" wailed Vince.

"Hey, don't run away!" growled Toothcarver, his voice becoming fainter. "I only want to play!"

"I think we're out-running him," said James, gasping for breath. "He's huge, so he can't dodge between the trees like we can."

Vince tripped over a loop-shaped root and crashed to the ground. James stopped to help him up. The poor vampire was splattered from head to foot in mud.

"Hang on," said James, pointing at a narrow gap in the trees. "Look! I think we've found the dragon's den."

A single shaft of daylight shone on a giant network of snapped-off branches. They'd been woven together into a spherical shape, and outside the den's round entrance was a doormat with the words **"YOU'RE NOT WELCOME, GO AWAY!"** on it.

James and Vince crept inside. The place smelt of stale meat and old socks.

"I reckon this is the last place he'll look for us," said James.

To one side of the den was a tall pile of bones. Every skull had been stripped of all its teeth. Beside a stone fireplace was a shelf on which dozens of tiny white figures were neatly arranged.

Wow, they're carved from his victims' teeth," said James. "There's a knight, and a princess, and I think that's a clown. You wouldn't think he could do such delicate work, with those whacking great claws."

Vince shrugged. "He's got to live up to his name, I guess. Good thing he's not called Bonecrunch."

Suddenly, a huge claw shot through the entrance to the den and snatched them both up.

"My middle name *isssss* Bonecrunch," cried the dragon in triumph. "Yum yum, it's time for lunch!"

James and Vince were held tightly in Toothcarver's grip. There was no escape.

"Mmm, vampires are ssssso tassssssty!" slurped the dragon. "There's no time to wasssssty." He slopped out his enormous forked tongue, and gave James's face a big wet lick.

Instantly, the dragon dropped the two friends to the ground and pulled a face. "Eurghh! Urghh! That's not vampire! It's a trick. Rrrrgh! Ooo, I'm going to be sssssick!" Spitting and retching, Toothcarver rushed away into the depths of the forest.

"That's the other thing I'd forgotten," grinned Vince. "Dragons can't *stand* the taste of humans."

James scraped the dragon drool off his face. "Lucky I was here, then," he croaked weakly as he rose to his feet.

"Hey! What's that you were sitting on?" exclaimed Vince.

Half buried in the heaped leaves and roots of the forest floor outside Toothcarver's den was a stone slab. It was about the size of a paperback book, and was pitted and lichen-covered with age. On it was carved, in tiny, worn and faded letters:

IF FEED'N'GULP YE SEEK TO MAKE

THESE THREE INGREDIENTS
YE MUST BAKE

HEAT A POT OF GOBLIN'S DROOL

AND MIX IN TOENAILS FROM
A TROLL

THE BREW'S COMPLETE WHEN IN
THE POT IS LAID

A SCALE FROM THE TAIL OF
A REAL MERMAID

"Yeeugh," James grimaced. "That really *is* disgusting."

Actually, it doesn't taste as bad as you might think," replied Vince. "Not mixed with a bit of apple juice. Trouble is, where are we going to get all these things?"

"I think I can help you there," piped up a voice from behind them.

The boys swung around and James pointed his torch into the gloom.

Chapter 5

Goblinton

James and Vince could hardly believe their eyes. Something appeared to be growing at great speed out of the nearest tree trunk. Two arms ending in twiggy fingers, two spindly legs, and a head formed from strips of bark. Two large green eyes gazed intently at them.

"What are you?" said James. "If you don't mind my asking."

"My name is Leafglade," said the creature in a high, wavering voice. She seemed to shimmer in the air, as if she might vanish at any moment. "I am a wood sprite. And this is my forest. But it's no place for strangers like you. Toothcarver will return soon and he'll be angry. He's been nibbling on nothing but roots and berries since last August."

"Well he's not eating either of us, is he V–" James paused as he felt the tickle of hot breath on his neck. He turned to find Vince standing very close behind him, looking extremely pale and twitching slightly.

"Is your friend unwell?" asked the wood sprite.

"Sort of," replied James.

Vince flashed his fangs. His eyes blazed red! "Getting reeeeeally hungry now," he groaned.

Thinking quickly, James fumbled in his bag. He pulled out the garlic he'd brought with him and shoved it at his friend. Vince coughed and stumbled back, shaking his head. At last, he returned to normal. Or, at least, as normal as he was going to get until he got some Feed'N'Gulp."

"That was close," said Vince sadly. "A whiff of that stuff is…well…it puts you right off your grub."

"Time's running short," said James. "Leafglade, you said you could help us?"

"Yes, I can show you where to find one of the ingredients you seek," she said. "The sooner you leave this forest, the better. Come, follow me."

She waved her hand, and the gnarled trunk of a tree opened up like a pair of curtains parting. She led the two friends down into a narrow passageway.

Spidery roots poked through the earth above them, and worms wriggled in the soil walls. The only light came from luminous fungus, which grew in streaks and lumps underfoot. Everywhere, there was a smell of wet earth and rotting vegetation.

"Umm, nice place you've got here," said James, trying to be polite.

"You think so?" smiled Leafglade. "Most humans think it's wet and horrid."

They made their way through many shadowy, winding tunnels. James quickly lost all sense of direction. He realized he'd never find his way out without Leafglade's help. It dawned on him that they were putting a lot of trust in a complete stranger.

At long last, the wood sprite reached up and pushed at a round metal hatch. "Up we go!" she cried.

The three of them emerged into the middle of a city. James and Vince gasped with surprise. It was night, and the honking of traffic filled the air. Giant jagged skyscrapers scattered with lights loomed overhead. Broken neon signs blinked. A steady rain pattered along the pavements, which were littered with rubbish.

It was the dirtiest place James had ever seen.

"Eurgh, where are we?" he said. "And is that mould growing up that building?"

"This is Goblinton," declared Leafglade. "It's smelly, it's filthy, it's loud and it's extremely unsafe, but it's also the only source of goblin's drool between here and Eville. Which is much worse, believe me."

Along a nearby flyover zoomed a bad tempered mass of goblin cars, most of them made from old bits of wood and sticky tape. Goblin pedestrians lolloped about here and there, picking their noses and scratching their bottoms. Goblin children, up way past their bedtime, squabbled and threw things at each other. They were slimy creatures, with bald heads and down-turned mouths.

"This one looks as if he might help us," said Leafglade, indicating a sneery old goblin who was sitting outside a cafe sipping a cup of warm mud and eating a slice of muck cake. The sign above the cafe read:

"Picksqueeze's Eatery – Nastiest Menu In Goblinton. Guaranteed."

"How do we make a horrible thing like that hand over some of his drool?" whispered Vince.

"You'll see," James replied.

Chapter 6

"To the King of the Goblins!"

James walked boldly up to the old goblin. "Excuse me," he said politely. "I wonder if I could ask a small favour of you?"

The goblin burped loudly. The smell made James's eyes sting. "No," grunted the goblin. "I'm 'aving me cake."

"Just a teeny tiny favour?" asked James, in the same voice he used when asking his parents for expensive birthday presents. "It won't take a minute."

The goblin glared at him. Then he glared at Vince. Then he glared at Leafglade. "No," he grunted. "Get lost."

"We haven't got anything to collect the drool in anyway," whispered Vince to James. "It's quite strong stuff, you know, you need a plastic container, or something similar."

James had an idea. He took the bag of sweets from his pocket, emptied the contents into Vince's hands, and held up the bag. "This is made of foil or something. Will that do?"

"Yes, that should be fine," Vince replied, "but–"

Suddenly, there was a splat as the old goblin dropped his muck cake on the ground. His lop-sided eyes were almost poking out on stalks.

"Is…" he stammered, "is them… *sweeties*?" He stared, a huge grin spreading across his thin mouth.

"Er, yes," said James. "Krispo Krunchies, I think. And maybe a few Choccie Blobs mixed in."

Dribble began to drip from the goblin's horrible grin. He shuffled towards Vince, his sticky green talons reaching out for the sweets.

"Ooo, I loves me sweeties," he spluttered through a cascade of spit. "Lemme have 'em. I want 'em! Better than stupid muck cake, I say."

"J-James!" cried Vince, backing away slowly. "The bag!"

James held the empty sweet packet out at arm's length under the goblin's dripping chin. The creature's drool soon filled it to the brim! James tied the top into a knot and carefully stashed the packet away in his bag.

Vince, terrified of getting his hand bitten, quickly tipped the sweets into the goblin's sticky palms. He stuffed all the sweets into his mouth in one huge, snuffling gulp. His face bulged as he chewed them up, chocolate-coated saliva escaping from his lips.

"That's the most disgusting thing I've ever seen," groaned Vince. "Come on, we've got what we came for, let's get out of here."

James and Vince turned to leave, and collided with six more goblins. Big ones. With clubs and catapults.

"Goin' somewhere?" sneered the tallest one.

The shortest one threw a handful of grubby coins at Leafglade. "Thanks, little miss," he smiled, showing a row of broken teeth. "Two human prisoners earn six groans."

James stared at Leafglade in dismay. "You double-crossed us?" he cried.

The wood sprite looked upset, but before she could answer, James and Vince found themselves seized in the goblins' slimey grip.

"To the King Of The Goblins!" cried the tallest one, raising his club high above his head.

"All hail, the King of the Goblins!" croaked the second tallest one, swinging his catapult.

"Ain't no goblin," muttered the shortest one to himself. "We all know 'e's a troll really – ARGHH!" he cried as the club crashed down on his head. He stuck out his tongue and blew a horrible, slimy raspberry at his attacker.

"Psssst!" Leafglade whispered to James. "Listen, I can get you out of this. Trust me."

Chapter 7

Troll Trouble

James leaned over to Leafglade and whispered "The trouble is, I don't trust you."

"I didn't betray you – brownie's promise," she replied, twizzling her hand in the air. "The Goblins just *assumed* you were my prisoners."

"What do you reckon Vince?" James asked, turning to his friend. But the vampire just shrugged his shoulders, his eyes squeezed shut. Vince's fangs were almost at full length now. Very soon he'd be so thirsty that he wouldn't be able to stop himself biting someone! So he had decided to concentrate as hard as he could on the whole Feed'N'Gulp recipe problem.

"OK, then Leafglade," James hissed. "Get us out of here."

"Oh goblins! Goblins!" Leafglade called out. "Before you leave, I'd like to thank you for rewarding me with the groans. Please allow me to sing you a song."

The goblins looked at each other. Hmm, they didn't normally approve of music.

"Yeah, alright," said the tallest goblin. "As long as it's a song about beheading."

The other goblins nodded and grunted in approval.

Leafglade smiled and began to sing. She sang so beautifully, so delicately, and with such musical grace that every last goblin began to cry.

"T-T-That's lovely, that is," sniffed the tallest goblin.

"Reminds me of me muvver's lullabies," blubbed the next tallest.

"It's a 'Yes' from me," sobbed the shortest, "she's through to the next round."

Before Leafglade had even got as far as the second verse, the goblins were sitting down hugging each other and bawling into the sleeves of their muck-covered coats. Without stopping her song, Leafglade indicated for James and Vince to creep away.

James nodded. He mouthed a sincere "thank you" to her, and she pointed back at the hatch through which they'd arrived in Goblinton.

James, taking one of the goblins' pointed clubs with him, quickly led Vince to safety (because Vince still had his eyes shut). He pulled open the metal hatch and pushed Vince into it, following behind. As they landed in the earthy tunnel, Vince's eyes popped open.

"Wh–why have you g–got that wooden stake? Aaargh, you're not g–going to…?" He started yelping and backing off.

"No, don't be silly!" cried James, shoving the weapon in his bag. "I'd never do that. I stole this from the goblins – for protection. Come on, let's get moving. They might come after us!"

James and Vince made their way along the smelly path which twisted and turned this way and that. They tried to remember the route Leafglade had taken, but it was impossible. Suddenly, a doorway appeared before them. James opened it slowly, peered outside, then quietly stepped through.

"Well, it looks as if we're just outside Goblinton," he said. The lights of the city flickered before them and behind them, steep cliffs dropped away to a stormy sea. Tufty grass sprouted in feeble clumps. Above them, the night sky was thick with rumbling clouds.

"Well," huffed Vince. "I don't think we'll find the King of the Goblins here!"

"What did you want to meet *him* for?" asked James.

"You weren't listening were you?" said Vince. "One of those goblins back there mentioned that the king is really a troll…Ring any bells…? The recipe?"

James slapped his forehead. "We need a troll's toenails."

"Exactly!" said Vince. "If we'd gone with the goblins, we'd have had those toenails right in front of us! Now we're on our own again! We don't even know where the nearest troll is!"

"What about that one over there?" pointed James.

Vince spun around.

Sitting on the cliff edge some distance away was a huge, green troll. He looked like half a dozen balls of mouldy dough squashed together, with weird swivelling eyes blinking above a wide mouth.

"While I was thinking," whispered Vince, "I came up with a plan. Trolls turn to stone when daylight strikes them, right?"

"Er, right," replied James.

"All we've got to do is keep this one talking until sunrise – it can't be long now. Once he's started turning to stone, we just snip off his toenails and we can be off! Trolls are so daft, it should be easy."

"That's a brilliant plan," said James.

They tip-toed over to the troll.

Suddenly the giant creature began to sniff.

"Feedle-fidle-fodle-foy, I smell the blood of a human boy!" He turned and snatched James into the air with his gigantic fist.

Chapter 8

The Riddle Fiddle

"Hello," said the troll, in a voice like half a pot of yoghurt slurping down a sink. "And who do we have here then?"

James decided he ought to speak slowly and carefully. Trolls in stories were always very, very stupid, with the intelligence of a squished flea.

"Hello…Mr…Troll…my…name… is…James."

"Delighted to meet you, dear boy," said the troll.

"Please don't hurt him," shouted Vince. "We're on a quest, you see… a very important quest."

"A quest you say?" said the troll, turning to look at Vince. "What sort of a quest."

"A *secret* quest," Vince said.

"Oh dear," said the troll. "Well, if you're not going to tell me about it, I'll just have to eat juicy James here!" The troll thrust James towards his big, smelly, open mouth.

"No, no…WAIT!" squawked Vince. "I *will* tell you the secret…of course I will…but you have to answer some riddles first. That's…that's the rule I'm afraid."

"Oh, goody!" cried the troll. "A quiz! I got to the semi-finals of *Brain Of Trolldom* on Troll-TV last year."

"Brilliant!" said Vince. "Well, here goes…what's black and white and red all over?"

"Hmm," mused the troll. "Tricky one. Anything to do with history? The Elfish-Dwarf Alliance of 1832? Or science? Isaac Ogre's Three Laws Of Grumbling?"

"Nope," said Vince.

"Hmm," said the troll. "Don't tell me, don't tell me…let me think…."

Vince managed to keep the troll guessing for quite a while.

"No, I give up," he said at last.

"An embarrassed zebra," said Vince.

The troll stared blankly at him for a moment. Then he got the joke. Then he couldn't stop laughing. He waved his arms about until James, still clutched in the troll's fist, became quite dizzy.

"I see! Black and white and red all over! An embarrassed Zebra! That's very good!"

"Or, it could be a penguin covered in ketchup," said Vince.

The troll howled with laughter. "Yes! Yes! Or, a skunk in raspberry jam!"

"Right," said Vince. "Here's the next riddle…what can catch but not throw?"

"Well that's easy!" said the troll. "A flibbergat!"

"A what?" James and Vince asked in unison.

"You know, a flibbergat!" said the troll, raising his eyebrows. "We always have a flibbergat on the Trollian cricket team. Never miss a catch…but useless bowlers. *Everybody* knows that!"

"Um…ok," said Vince.

"Ah," said the troll, as the sun began to appear on the horizon. "I see it's almost time for me to go. Can't be out after sun-up or I turn to stone, you know. So come on…tell me about your secret quest, and then I'll decide whether to have juicy James for breakfast."

"But I have one more riddle left," said Vince. "It's the best one yet!"

"Hmm, ok," said the troll. "Just one more."

"What comes once in a minute, twice in a moment, but never in a thousand years?" asked Vince.

"Ooh I say," said the troll. "That's an excellent riddle. Ummm…a second? No, no, that's silly…er…*once* in a minute…ooh dear…."

Vince watched as shafts of sunlight crept across the raging sea below the cliff.

"No, I don't know," said the troll, getting to his feet. "You'll have to tell me the answer."

"But you haven't had a proper guess yet!" replied Vince.

"Tell me…NOW!" bellowed the troll.

"Oh ok then," said Vince as the troll towered over him. "The answer is… let me see…What comes once in a minute, twice in a moment, but never in a–"

"TELL ME THE ANS–"

The troll stopped mid-sentence. Before James and Vince's eyes, as daybreak burst upon them, the troll's face began to turn cold and grey.

James managed to pull the club from his bag and whacked the troll's hand. It opened, dropping James to the ground.

"Quick! The toenails!" cried James. He grabbed his penknife and threw it to Vince.

Vince began to saw at the first nail as James rushed over.

"Hurry!" cried James as the stony greyness edged down the troll's leg.

"I'm going as quickly as I can," said Vince dropping a couple of toenails into James's bag.

Suddenly, there was a mighty cracking sound. "Wow, that was a big toenail," said James.

"That didn't come from the troll," croaked Vince nervously. "That came from beneath us."

The immense weight of a solid stone troll was too much for the cliff edge to bear. Without warning, it suddenly gave way! James and Vince fell fifty metres or more, splashing into the freezing cold sea at the base of what was left of the cliff.

They surfaced coughing and spluttering. Waves rolled all around them. To their amazement, they were both completely unhurt.

"Wow, that was a lucky escape," gasped James, flicking his wet hair out of his eyes.

Close by, the surface of the sea suddenly exploded! Something huge rose up, and up, and up out of the water.

"Oh no, the legends are true!" wailed Vince.

"What is it?" cried James.

Chapter 9

The Monster and the Mermaid

Out of the water rose the biggest creature James had ever seen. It towered up over the surface of the sea like a huge mass of wriggling rubber. Water cascaded off its glistening surface. The monster's domed head was studded with dozens of eyes and surrounded by a writhing ring of tentacles.

"We're close to the shores of Woe here!" cried Vince. "That must be the octosquid which lives in Grimsleeth's Cave!"

"What's that it's holding?" yelled James.

The monster gave a slobbering, gurgly roar. The thing it was holding let out an almighty, high-pitched scream.

Clutched in the monster's suckery grip was a small figure. Struggling to keep afloat, James gazed up and blinked. The person, if that's what it was, had pale skin and very long, seaweedy hair. But that wasn't what caught his attention. It was the long, fishy tail, flicking and flapping in a desperate attempt to escape.

"Is that a *mermaid?*" cried James. "A real mermaid?"

Then he thought for a moment and shook his head. "Why am I surprised, after all the weird things that have happened today?" he muttered to himself.

The mermaid hammered on the monster's tentacle with both fists, but to no avail. She called the monster a long list of rude names, but that didn't help either.

"Wow, that's a tough little mermaid," said Vince.

"We have to save her!" James urged, as a huge wave washed them within touching distance of the monster.

"Unfortunately, I think it might be too late," replied Vince. "It's about to bite off her head!"

The creature raised the mermaid up level with its beaky mouth. Her scaly tail thrashed, and she tried giving the creature a really nasty pinch.

It paused for a moment and winced. Then it glared at her with every last one of its eyes. She glared right back at it. "Eat me then," she cried defiantly, "and I hope I give you dreadful tummy ache!"

James had an idea. "If a pinch can make that monster think twice," he said to Vince, "let's see what a jab on a tentacle will do! Chuck me that penknife."

Vince had almost forgotten he was still clutching the tool he'd used to trim the troll's toenails. He tossed it to James, who managed to catch it, just before it plopped into the sea.

The monster's huge, wiggling tentacles were barely an arm's length away. Vince didn't want to look. He hated animal cruelty – even if the animal in question was a deadly, gigantic, ravenous beast.

The octosquid opened its beak-like mouth. A horrible smell of fish and chewed-up pirates wafted out. The mermaid scowled and held her nose.

James lunged through the surf and jabbed at the monster's rubbery flesh with his penknife. The blade bounced off! He tried again, only harder this time. It was no good! The monster hadn't even noticed. The mermaid screamed with fright as the monster drew her closer and closer to its dreadful, clack-clacking beak.

"I know!" cried James. "Vince! Bite it! Your fangs are really long and sharp now! Quick, before that poor mermaid becomes dinner!"

"I can't do that!" wailed Vince. "It's cruel! And besides, I don't like seafood!"

"You're her only hope!" cried James. "Just one little nibble…pleeeease."

"OK," replied his friend. "I *would* love to bite something right now!"

Vince grabbed one of the beast's waving limbs and sank his fangs into it. At once, the monster yelped and dropped the mermaid into the sea.

For a moment, the octosquid bobbed on the choppy waves, its many eyes blinking. Then a gush of air began to escape from the two punctures Vince's fangs had made.

There was a long, loud, rather rude sound. The monster lifted right out of the sea, whizzing round and round above their heads as it shrank down, and down, and down, like a burst balloon. Finally it came to rest on the water's surface right in front of them, its tentacles narrow and saggy, its eyes blinking helplessly.

Within seconds, the monster had gone from being the size of half a mountain to the size of a small boulder. James and Vince stared at it in disbelief. The octosquid glared back at them in embarrassment. It went red around the beak, and swam away as fast as it could, squeaking in disgust.

Chapter 10

Fangtastic!

The mermaid glided gracefully through the water to James. "You saved my life!" she cried, in a tinkly, watery voice. "How can I *ever* repay your kindness?"

"Umm, well," said James. "We're on a quest to save my friend here from turning all bloodthirsty. We've got nearly everything we need, but we're just short of the final ingredient."

"I see," said the mermaid. "And what is it?"

"Well, actually," began James. "We need some scales from the tail of a real mermaid."

"Oh dear," groaned the mermaid. "That sounds painful."

"Well we did just save you from the jaws of a sea monster!" Vince pointed out.

"True," replied the mermaid. "Help yourself…but be gentle." She flipped her tail up above the water's surface.

"Ooh…ow…oof!" the mermaid winced, as James plucked three scales and put them into his bag.

"The vampires of the world will be very grateful," grinned James. "Come on, Vince, zap us home!"

"Not a moment too soon," mumbled Vince. "I'm very cold and horribly hungry."

* * *

Thanks to Vince's amazing vampire powers, the boys were soon standing in James's back garden. It was sunset, and as daylight faded on the horizon, Vince's family emerged from next door. They were dressed in black from head to toe. Their fangs glinted in the moonlight and they looked famished.

"Eek!" shrieked Vince. "We're just in time! They need Feed'N'Gulp right now, before it's too late!"

He ran up to his parents. "Mum! Dad! We've got the long-lost recipe! *And* the secret ingredients!"

James hurried over. Inside his bag, safe and sound, were the goblin's drool, troll's toenails and mermaid's scales. Without them noticing, he pulled out the bulb of garlic again and stuck it in his pocket…just in case!

"Quick! Into the kitchen!" gasped Vince's mum. "Dad, you get a pan of water on the boil. Vince, mix up a nice sauce we can cook the ingredients in. James, run down the street and tell the Batsbys at No. 38 to stop chasing humans and come over. We'll have the Feed'N'Gulp ready in a few minutes."

Less than half an hour later, Vince was pouring the warm, soupy contents of a large cooking pot into a series of mugs. Gathered around the kitchen table were vampires from all over town. James gazed around at them all, wondering if he should have brought a few more bulbs of garlic.

"Here goes!" said Vince. He drank his mug down in one go. "Mmm, different from the old stuff. Tastier. Sort of tomato flavoured."

James watched in amazement as his friend's fangs began to retreat. Vince's skin stopped looking like ancient parchment, and his eyes became less red and boggly.

"It works!" cried James.

All the vampires slurped their Feed'N'Gulp, laughing and cheering. Vince hurried to the computer in the living room and posted the recipe online. Vampires everywhere, who'd been waiting nervously for James and Vince to return from their quest, breathed a sigh of relief.

Over the following weeks and months, James and Vince became

heroes to the legions of the undead. The world's goblins, trolls and mermaids suddenly found themselves being offered well-paid employment, supplying drool, toenails and scales in nicely packaged economy-sized bags. The vampire community began cooking Feed'N'Gulp for themselves at home, and pretty soon there were variations on the basic formula that every creature of the night was simply dying to try.

James and Vince wrote about their adventures in a book, with recipes. It became a big hit. Nobody believed that the story they told was true, of course. Well, nobody human, that is....

THE END

FICTION EXPRESS

THE READERS TAKE CONTROL!

Have you ever wanted to change the course of a plot, change a character's destiny, tell an author what to write next?

Well, now you can!

'The Vampire Quest' was originally written for the award-winning interactive e-book website Fiction Express.

Fiction Express e-books are published in gripping weekly episodes. At the end of each episode, readers are given voting options to decide where the plot goes next. They vote online and the winning vote is then conveyed to the author who writes the next episode, in real time, according to the readers' most popular choice.

www.fictionexpress.co.uk

WINNER
Education Resources
Award for Innovation

FICTION EXPRESS

TALK TO THE AUTHORS

The Fiction Express website features a blog where readers can interact with the authors while they are writing. An exciting and unique opportunity!

FANTASTIC TEACHER RESOURCES

Each weekly Fiction Express episode comes with a PDF of teacher resources packed with ideas to extend the text.

"The teaching resources are fab and easily fill a whole week of literacy lessons!"
Rachel Humphries, teacher at Westacre Middle School

FICTI●N EXPRESS

The Rise of the Rabbits
by Barry Hutchison

When twins Harvey and Lola are given the school rabbit, Mr Lugs, to look after for the weekend, they're both very excited. That is until the rabbit begins to mutate and decides the time has come for bunnies to rise up and seize control.

It's up to Harvey and Lola to find a way to return Mr Lugs and his friends to normal, before the menaces sweep across the country – and then the world!

ISBN 978-1-78322-540-8

FICTI●N EXPRESS

The Sand Witch
by Tommy Donbavand

When twins Chris and Ella are left to look after their younger brother on a deserted beach, they expect everything to be normal, boring in fact. But then something extraordinary happens! Will the Sand Witch succeed in passing on her sandy curse in this exciting adventure?

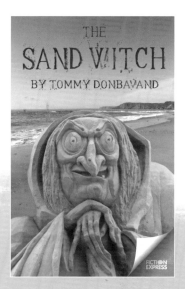

ISBN 978-1-78322-544-6

Simon Cheshire

Simon Cheshire is an award-winning children's writer who has been visiting schools, libraries and literary festivals for well over a decade. He's done promotional book tours around various parts of the UK and America, he's written and presented a number of radio programmes, but he has yet to achieve his ambition of going to the Moon.

Simon was a dedicated reader from a very young age, and started writing stories when he was in his teens. After he turned thirty and finally accepted he'd always have the mind of a ten-year-old, he began creating children's stories and at last found his natural habitat. Since his first book appeared in 1997, his work has been published in various countries and languages around the world.

He's written for a broad range of ages, but the majority of his work is what he calls "action-packed comedies" for 8-12 year-olds. He lives in Warwick with his wife and children, but spends most of his time in a world of his own.